95

DI

BICYCLE MOTOCROSS RACING

BICYCLE
MOTOCROSS
RACING

TOM MORAN

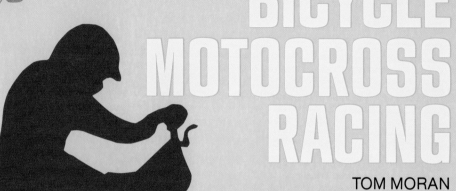

Lerner Publications Company ▪ Minneapolis, Minnesota

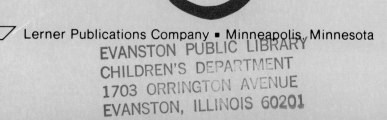

ACKNOWLEDGMENTS: The photographs are reproduced through the courtesy of: pp. 4, 11, 16, 21, 24, 32, 34, 39, 47, Brad Fanshaw; pp. 5, 6, 26, 30, 31, 37, 46, *ABA Action;* pp. 8, 12, 18, 20, 38, 43, Denny Griffiths; p. 9, Art Thomas; p. 10, *Super BMX*/BMX Products; pp. 14, 15, 27, 28, 36, 42, 44, *Bicycles and Dirt;* p. 22, Red Line Engineering; p. 40, BMX Products.

The author would like to express his thanks to the following individuals and organizations: Fran Durst, National Bicycle League; Brad Fanshaw, Competition Publications; Byron Friday, Scorpion Cycle; Clayton John, American Bicycle Association; Betty Korf, Red Line Engineering; Richard Lee; Russ Okawa, BMX Products; Eric Rube; Fred Teeman, Schwinn Bicycle Company.

LIBRARY OF CONGRESS CATALOGING IN PUBLICATION DATA

Moran, Tom.
  Bicycle motocross racing.

  (Superwheels & thrill sports)
  Summary: Describes various aspects of bicycle motocross racing including the history of the sport, the equipment, tracks, rules, safety, tactics, and the racing organizations.
    1. Bicycle motocross—Juvenile literature.
  [1. Bicycle motocross] I. Title. II. Series.
  GV1049.3.M673 1986   796.6   85-23997
  ISBN 0-8225-0510-X (lib. bdg.)

Manufactured in the United States of America.

International Standard Book Number: 0-8225-0510-X
Library of Congress Catalog Card Number: 85-23997

1 2 3 4 5 6 7 8 9 10 94 93 92 91 90 89 88 87 86

CONTENTS

INTRODUCTION **7**

THE HISTORY OF BMX RACING **9**

THE BMX MACHINE **13**

THE TRACK:
FROM START TO FINISH **17**

BMX SAFETY **23**

ORGANIZED BMX RACING **29**

RACETIME! **35**

BMX RACING TACTICS **41**

THE FUTURE OF BMX RACING **45**

When the starting gate drops, it's time for full pedal power!

INTRODUCTION

Practice is over. This race is for real. Poised on their bicycles, a line of racers waits at the top of the starter's hill. These racers have already survived three hotly contested elimination races, and their top finishes have qualified them for the afternoon's championship sprint.

"Racers ready!" shouts the starter. A brief silence follows as the racers wait for the starting signal.

As the steel starting gate crashes to the ground, a control light flashes green, unleashing the pack of racers. The cyclists blaze down the steep slope, straining against their pedals and fighting to establish the best position in the first turn.

The colorful array of racing uniforms, bicycles, and helmets becomes a blur as the racers accelerate through a series of rough bumps. From vantage points along the track, spectators cheer loudly for friends and favorite racers. A voice over the loudspeaker announces the names of the leaders as the racers bunch together around a steeply banked turn.

It is this fierce competition and fast-paced excitement that has made *bicycle motocross*, often called *BMX*, such an immensely popular youth sport. Even though bicycle motocross is a less costly alternative, BMX racers can experience the same thrills as participants in motorcycle, minicycle, and other motorized racing sports.

BMX appeals to people at all levels of racing experience from five-year-old novices, barely able to balance their small bicycles, to world-class professionals, whose skills have been tested and refined from years of competition. The broad-based appeal of BMX brings racers, parents, and spectators out to local tracks to sample its thrills week after week.

Earning a first-place "Number One" plate is every BMX racer's dream.

THE HISTORY OF BMX RACING

Considering that not many years ago there were neither BMX bicycles nor organized races for their riders, BMX has grown at a phenomenal rate. BMX competition now flourishes in Europe, the United States, South America, South Africa, Australia, and Japan, and several national and world-class championship races are staged each year at sites around the world.

BMX racing began in the early 1970s when the Schwinn Bicycle Company introduced its *Sting Ray* model. This small bike was tremendously popular with young riders. Before long, the more daring riders began to imitate the stunts and styles of motorcycle motocross racers, testing their skills at maneuvering through jumps, mud hazards, and other obstacles set up in empty sandlots or on neighborhood trails. The young sport gained exposure when BMX racers began to compete on motorcycle and minibike tracks, often as a preliminary to the motorized races.

The *Sting Ray* bicycle was the first BMX racer.

A wide turn means extra-fast action on the track.

Gradually, this new form of non-motorized bicycle racing became more formally organized. Tracks designed solely for BMX racing first appeared in southern California, and the sport rapidly expanded into other regions of the United States: the Southwest, the South, and the East. Eventually, associations of BMX riders began to organize regional, national, and international competitions and to establish uniform rules for track operation, safety, and racing standards. Bicycle manufacturers, BMX equipment dealers, and other youth-oriented businesses sponsored races, BMX clinics, and racing teams to promote their own products and the sport of BMX as well. Commercial interest in BMX also created a professional group of expert racers who traveled throughout the world, endorsing manufacturers' products and acting as BMX ambassadors.

Today, BMX has truly entered the major league of youth sports. Movies, televised sports coverage, and articles in major magazines and newspapers have all contributed to its popularity and its soaring growth.

Even young riders can participate in BMX racing, a sport for all ages.

A BMX bicycle must be sturdy enough for rough riding yet lightweight for easy handling.

THE BMX MACHINE

A reliable bicycle is the most important part of BMX racing. Riders must have bikes that can withstand the tremendous physical punishment of BMX competition. Contenders cannot afford to suffer equipment failure—a chain that snaps on the final straightway, a crank pedal that fractures when leg power is applied, or handlebars that slip in the gooseneck—during the critical seconds of a race.

The BMX bicycle is a hybrid machine. Although its most elementary features resemble a traditional street bike with balloon tires, a closer look reveals a sophisticated racing machine with its own unique design features.

BMX bicycles are smaller and more compact than street bikes or European-styled multi-speeds. Most have 20-inch wheels, although smaller bicycles, called *minis*, have 16-inch wheels, and larger *cruiser* bicycles have 26-inch wheels.

Today's BMX bicycle evolved rapidly from the old Schwinn *Sting Ray*. The early sandlot competitions had tested their durability with high-speed jumps and collisions that subjected the bicycle's frames, forks, rims, axles, goosenecks, and handlebars to grueling strain. Manufacturers responded with innovative changes in the bicycle's design and construction, giving it added strength to keep prized bikes from suddenly turning into useless scrap metal. That quality is constantly improving as manufacturers find new designs and materials that change the look, feel, and performance of the BMX racing machine.

This rider knows the importance of keeping her bicycle in top condition.

The latest models of BMX racing bikes have been designed for reliable performance, and their components are reinforced to stand up under the rigors of the track. They usually have a stronger closed (boy's style) frame with thicker front forks, longer cranks, and thicker materials at high stress points. Extra strength is also achieved by sophisticated metal joining and welding processes, and quality sealed bearings help to keep the moving parts in working order in the dusty, gritty BMX environment.

Although strength is a priority, BMX manufacturers and racers are also concerned with the weight of the bicycle. Serious racers want their bikes to be as light as possible so they will be quicker and more responsive. Consequently, bicycle designers are using some of the same lightweight materials that are being used in motor car racing and in the aerospace industry, including chrome-moly steel, titanium, graphite, special high-strength plastics, magnesium, and rugged forged aluminum alloys. These materials have been used successfully to achieve lighter weight without sacrificing strength.

BMX racing bicycles are now manufactured and distributed worldwide, and there are models for all skill levels and budgets. Young riders who expect to do more street riding than competitive racing can buy less expensive BMX-styled bicycles and beginners' competition models. There is also a wide range of moderately priced bicycles for the intermediate level racer.

Bike shops and advertisements in BMX magazines offer special parts and accessories that riders can add to their bikes to make them lighter, stronger, or faster. Some racers assemble their own customized bicycles from individual components, and pre-assembled custom-made racing bikes are also available to serious competitors who are willing to pay premium prices.

High-flying "hot dog" jumpers put plenty of air between themselves and the ground!

As they round a corner, two racers fight to get a grip in the loose dirt.

THE TRACK: FROM START TO FINISH

The track is the stage where the high-powered drama of BMX is acted out. It can be a large commercial facility with modern lighting, grandstands, and electronic starting equipment or a temporary course built by local volunteers.

During the sport's infancy, BMX tracks were usually makeshift operations. Some races were held on motorcycle tracks, but most took place on vacant lots, in parks, or in other temporary racing areas. Many of these roughly erected tracks were nothing more than long downhill stretches through rugged terrain. Hay bales, discarded automobile tires, and rope marked the course and attempted to separate the handful of spectators from the action. Elastic bands and rubber hoses restrained the riders at the starting line and prevented any of them from getting a head start. The races were organized by community volunteers and parents who acted as the race officials.

As BMX began to grow in popularity, track facilities improved. Youth and civic organizations secured leases on park space and surplus land in order to expand their operations and to build more permanent racing homes. In response to the mushrooming interest in BMX, commercial track operations that charged entry fees to cover the cost of skilled crews of officials, organizers, and venders were eventually established.

Leading the pack is an enviable position for a BMX racer.

Whether the track is a professionally staffed facility or a temporary park site, its basic construction remains the same. Although there are unlimited variations, every BMX course must have a start, several turns, a variety of obstacles, and a finish line.

The start is usually at the top of a small hill or ramp, and the initial downward slope allows the racers to gain speed quickly. Racers assemble, side by side, behind the starting line until the starting signal is given. The race begins with a *massed start*. All the racers will begin at the same time, and the winner is the rider who crosses the finish line first.

Many facilities have electronically timed starting systems, which are often called *Christmas trees* because they signal the start of the race with flashing lights. Other race tracks have manually operated steel gates that are lowered to signal the official start. Well designed gates prevent jumped starts and keep the racers lined up with room between their handlebars.

Most race courses have multiple turns. This adds to the difficulty of the track and keeps the race confined to a smaller, more visible area. Some are hairpin turns that require a quick change of direction, and other wide sweeping turns hardly require any slowing down. Many turns are steeply banked, or sloped. These high dirt banks, called *berms*, permit the riders to zip through the turns at higher speeds.

Sudden dips in the track are one kind of obstacle that BMX riders frequently encounter during a race.

Between the turns, there are a variety of obstacles. When well planned, these obstacles add excitement to the course and offer a safe challenge for the racers. Obstacles like jumps, sudden drops, bumps, and other irregularities have acquired names such as *whoop de dos, table tops (TT's), doublers, moonwalkers, step jumps, offsets,* and *hump jumps.* These obstacles send bikes flying into the air and test the riders' skills, strategy, and timing. Mud and water hazards, which were very popular in the early days of BMX, are still found on the professional segments of some racing circuits.

Although a downhill course might be longer, tracks usually confine the racing action to a length of 800 to 1,400 feet (240-420 m). Many modern tracks are similar in shape and design and look like they have been built from the same mold. While some competitors criticize this lack of variety, others like the uniformity because it encourages racers to try different tracks and minimizes any home-track advantage for local racers.

Several recent track developments have made racing opportunities more accessible to riders and more exciting for spectators. Some facilities have built special segments of the track with more difficult obstacles and challenging turns for use by professional racers. Night lighting and indoor facilities have also greatly extended the opportunities to race and practice. Indoor facilities with all of the racing action, spectator seating, and other track services under one roof have been constructed in areas where seasonal bad weather shortens the outdoor racing season or where open space is at a premium.

BMX tracks are often lined with old tires or hay bales (page 22) to provide a safe and fairly soft barrier in case of spinouts.

During a race, BMX riders try to move as fast as possible without losing control of their bicycles.

BMX SAFETY

A bike slides out from beneath a racer on the side of a banked turn. The bicycle and rider bounce along the dirt and, in a cloud of dust, roll over the top of the berm. Another rider misjudges a jump and loses control in midair. She sails past the handlebars and hits the ground with a breath-wrenching thud that momentarily silences the crowd. Four racers skid around a hairpin turn. As one rider loses his balance and swerves into the other riders, all four racers are thrown to the ground. The confused mass of fallen bicycles and riders slides toward a hay bale at the track's edge, and race spotters quickly rush to assist them.

BMX racers often flip over their handlebars or fall. In the heat of competition, bicycles collide, riders crack elbows, and fallen racers get in the way of other cyclists. These collisions make BMX a thrilling spectator event, but they also reflect an element of danger. No BMX competitor is immune to bruises, scrapes, or abrasions, and these injuries are the price that all novices must pay while they learn the fundamentals of BMX. For expert riders, such injuries are less frequent.

While minor scrapes are common occurences, major injuries are rare in organized BMX competitions. Insurance statistics show that BMX is one of the safest contact sports. Its competitors, like national champion racer Eric Rupe, have suffered fewer serious injuries than participants of other sports.

"I've been racing over 10 years," says Rupe. "The only injury I've had is a sprained ankle, and I got that stepping off my bike."

Although serious injuries are rare in BMX racing, every racer can expect to "hit the dirt" at some time.

The sport's enviable safety record is the result of a carefully defined and strictly enforced safety program. By adhering to safety regulations and precautions, track operators and racers have guarded against serious injury.

All competitors must wear special apparel, including a helmet, mouthguard, and long pants. The thickly padded helmet must fit well, and its chin strap must always be fastened. Some riders prefer helmets with wraparound mouth and face guards, but other racers prefer separate face protectors, goggles, or visors.

Although regulations require long pants, shoes, and long-sleeved shirts or elbow pads, a racer's uniform is largely a matter of personal taste. Special racing suits with sewn-in padding at the thighs, rumps, and elbows are especially popular. Gloves and additional padding, such as rib protectors, are optional.

Racing bicycles, too, must comply with safely regulations. The top bar of the bicycle's frame, the crossbar on the handlebars, and the gooseneck must be padded to cushion against accidental bumps. Riders use either homemade taped padding or buy brightly colored snap-on pads. Rules also require that ends of the handlebars be covered with safety grips to eliminate the danger of gouges or "cookie cutter" type injuries, and other bike components cannot protrude unsafely. Axles, for example, can project no more than one-quarter inch beyond the frame's fork supports.

Rounding a wide sweeping turn, racers try to keep up with the lead rider.

A pre-race safety inspection makes sure that the safety standards are met and that all equipment is in good mechanical condition. Officials check the brakes—either caliper-type rear wheel brakes or coaster types—because responsive braking is vital in preventing pile-ups and unnecessary collisions.

Track operators help to insure the sport's safety by providing readily available emergency transportation and on-site first aid equipment. They also station spotters around the course to aid fallen riders. The combined efforts of the track operators and the racing participants have helped to minimize serious injuries without inhibiting fast, exciting BMX racing programs.

While the other racers speed toward the finish line, a spotter will quickly come on the track to assist the fallen rider.

Riders and crew line the track, awaiting the start of their motos.

ORGANIZED BMX RACING

Numerous local, regional, and national organizations plan and schedule BMX racing events. These organizations establish standards for track operations, set rules for racing and sportsmanship, provide insurance for participants, define racing classes, and keep track of standings for individual racers. The groups usually charge a membership fee and issue identification numbers to members for use during competition. Although these organizations sometimes compete against each other, BMX racers may join more than one organization.

The racing organizations classify competitors on the basis of skill level and performance.

Racers who have not yet won a race are called *beginners*. Those who have won at least one race but fewer than five are called *novices*. Competitors who have won five or more events are in the *expert* class.

The three rider skill classifications are divided into smaller racing classes established on the basis of age. Categories range from ages 5 and under to 17 and over. Competitors usually race only against other riders in their own age group.

Separate competition is also allowed for female racers. These classes are also divided by age and have attracted a growing number of highly skilled and competitive female racers.

Racers eagerly wait for their chance to try out the track.

Most tracks have set up separate classes for the larger cruiser-style bicycles. The 26-inch wheels of these bikes are favored by older riders who are often too large for the standard BMX cycles. Cruiser competition is also divided into age catagories. Separate classes begin with racers age 12 and younger and include divisions for older racers, adults, and parents. These "dads' races," sometimes jokingly called "cardiac classes," are very popular at many tracks.

The most competitive racers can advance into BMX's professional ranks. These riders receive prizes and money for winning motos, races, and various championships. It is here that the sport's top riders are found.

BMX racing attracts all kinds of fans!

This group of young racers is ready to climb up the starting hill and begin the next moto.

The youngest age at which a racer can become a professional is 14. The first year is usually spent racing in a beginning pro catagory. After gaining experience and winning sufficient prize money to show the ability to compete with the fastest riders, a racer may advance into the top pro class.

Pro riders compete on both cruisers and regular BMX bicycles, and the top pros travel to major races held at sites across the United States and Canada and throughout the world. These races are usually sponsored by a BMX equipment manufacturer.

The two largest BMX organizations in the United States are the American Bicycle Association (ABA) and the National Bicycle League (NBL). The ABA, founded in 1977, lists over 92,000 members and *sanctions,* or gives approval to, races conducted at more than 500 tracks in the United States. Each year, the ABA sponsors a Gold Cup Series as well as a series of races that culminates in a Grand National Championship race in November on Thanksgiving Day. Riders earn points for their finishes in these national races, and the ABA publishes their cumulative point scores in an association magazine called *ABA Action.* The ABA also publishes a BMX feature magazine, *Bicycles and Dirt.*

The NBL, which began in 1976, has over 30,000 members and sanctions more than 250 tracks throughout the United States and Canada. The NBL is affiliated with the International BMX Federation (IBmxF), which regulates international racing and world championship events. The NBL sponsors a national racing series called *War of the Stars.* The series climaxes with a Grand National race held each year on Labor Day weekend in September. Point standings for NBL racers are published in the league's magazine, *Bicycles Today.*

At race time, spectators, crew, and riders crowd alongside the track.

RACETIME!

On race day, a BMX track leaps to life with the pageantry, logistical problems, and nonstop action of a three-ring circus. Multicolored balloons and banners often decorate the track area, and spectators overflow the grandstand and spill out to lawn chairs along the course or on top of motor homes parked near the track. Fabric-topped pavilions, often emblazoned with sponsors' logos or advertisements, provide shelter and meeting places for racers, organizers, and the press. Huge crowds surround the refreshment, equipment, and souvenir stands.

The racers themselves have much to accomplish before the starting gate opens. Top racers begin planning their strategies early. They analyze the track and the competition and try to get the edge that will help them cross the finish line first.

In order to gain that advantage, a racer must know the track. Tracks permit practice sessions prior to the actual races, and all riders are on the course early to perfect their techniques. They practice many different methods of attacking turns and jumps, because they know that their rivals will not always let them use the fastest or most ideal route during the race. Riders test the inside and outside lines on each curve and berm. They attempt jumps at different speeds and from every possible angle and mentally note good places to attempt to pass should they trail during the race. The cyclists are learning the track—"dialing it in" —in preparation for the actual contest.

A lull in the day's activities gives riders a chance to share their racing experiences and talk about the next event.

As two young racers "ride the berm," a spotter and a race official keep an alert eye on the track.

During the practice laps, racers also keep an eye on their opponents. They watch how competitors approach the track and try to guess how they will react during the heat of the competition. Some riders will be familiar foes who have raced together many times before. Others will be strangers of unknown ability.

As racetime nears, the track becomes a beehive of activity. A swarm of racers pushes forward to get a glimpse of the race assignment sheet. The pit area hums as racers, aided by their parents and friends, make last minute adjustments to their bicycles. Other riders form dense packs as they inch their way uphill to the starting gate.

Good riders know they must clear a jump and get back on the ground as quickly as possible so they will not lose valuable seconds during a race.

As they wait, racers continue to plan strategies for the race ahead. The starting gate becomes more important as the racers move closer to their appointed starting times, and they mentally note how many seconds elapse before the green light flashes on for each race. In order to be ready to go when the gate finally drops open, they know they must have the starting system timed perfectly.

The pre-race preparations are extremely important. The race itself will last only a few brief seconds, and, during that short time, the action and stress will be so intense that every move must be automatic. When the starting gate falls open, the racers have no time left for making decisions; instead, they will have to react spontaneously. That is when the earlier preparations will pay off.

BMX racing action peaks repeatedly as wave after wave of riders surges from the starting gate in a series of mini-races that will ultimately culminate in a championship event. These mini-races are called *motos*. The course remains exactly the same for each moto, and the top individuals in the motos advance to the semi-final and main events.

Tracks use two different systems to advance racers to the higher rounds. Under the *moto system* used by the ABA, the winner of each moto automatically advances to the semi-main or main event and does not participate in any more motos. In the *transfer system* favored by the NBL, points are awarded to the top finishers of each moto. After all the motos have been run, racers with the highest point totals advance to the semi-main or main event.

The competition gains on the leader as she crosses-over coming off a jump.

When going over bumps and jumps, racers try to stay low to the ground.

BMX RACING TACTICS

Whether it is a preliminary moto or the championship event, the basic track action and strategies are the same. The racers explode out of the starting gate and fight for the lead. A good gate position may help, but pure pedaling power is more often the key to an early lead.

The leader going into the track's first turn has a tremendous advantage over the other racers. The leader can use his or her legs and bicycle position to control the racers who trail and to block those who threaten to pass. Unless she or he makes a mistake, it is difficult to pass a rider. Trailing racers keep pressure on the leader. The obstacles and turns are key places to force an error and pick up an advantage over contenders. "Hot doggers" may display the most spectacular jumps, but they lose precious seconds while they hang in the air. Instead, jumps are best navigated as close to the ground as possible in order to land quickly. Some riders use their high position on a berm to pass opponents by swooping down diagonally across the track. Other riders take *whoop do dos* at high speed to skim over the tops of the ridges instead of jolting through each depression. But at those speeds, riders have very little control of their bikes and could wipe out at any second.

The racers are crowded together, and the action is frantic, sometimes rough. The pack charges through the turns, and everyone looks for an opening to gain a few extra inches.

"You're banging elbows. Three or four guys might crash. It gets really physical," explains Eric Rupe, a world-class rider. "You have to be tough. You can't be stiff. A rider might get squirrelly and lean on you. You have to lean back and stay up. They really bang you. You're hurting. You're three abreast and on wide turns they might try to "T-bone" you, run you off the track. It's rough riding."

Turning corners sharply helps bikers to gain ground during a moto.

If no racer gains a clear early advantage, the lead may change many times. The bicycles seesaw back and forth, each inching ahead for a brief moment. Even the slightest mistake— a slipped pedal or judgment error—becomes a costly one.

Racers shift position, moving from the inside to the outside edge of the track, hoping for more space to power pedal ahead. They let the berms whip them around the turns, keeping the pressure on the leader at all times. Leg muscles begin to tire, and the racers gasp

Each rider uses a slightly different route to maneuver this bermed turn.

for air and reserve energy. But, relentlessly, they keep moving.

This action-packed drama continues all the way around the track. Some racers fall or momentarily lose control, and others swerve or "bunny hop" to avoid a pile up. Everyone quickly adjusts, and, without a second thought,

resumes the fight to the finish line. The goal is to get there first.

There is only one winner for each moto. If victory cannot be found this race day, the racers will continue to search for it tomorrow or the next week when BMX action starts up again.

Night racing has added to the popularity of BMX.

THE FUTURE OF BMX RACING

The growth of BMX has been explosive. A decade ago, few people could have imagined the phenomenal popularity and public exposure that the sport enjoys today.

According to industry estimates, BMX bicycles account for 30 to 47 percent of the new bicycles sold in the United States. BMX fashions, flashy sitckers and decals, and non-racing models of BMX-styled bicycles are also very popular. Cable and regular network television coverage of BMX activity on sports, news, and entertainment programs attest to the growing interest in the sport.

Some top professional and amateur riders have become youth celebrities and have appeared in print and television advertising. Several widely circulated BMX magazines feature articles about these stars and cater to the sport's fans and participants.

There are many reasons for the success of BMX. The sport was started by young riders, and, despite high levels of adult involvement at the administrative levels, it remains a youth activity. The bold images and vivid color associated with racers in uniform and their sparkling chrome machines has a natural allure. The sport offers an outlet to those with a daredevil's instinct, providing speed, jumps, and intense competition in a safe and controlled environment.

A quick start can make a big difference in the outcome of a close race.

BMX also survives because it is a form of family recreation. Parents and relatives are needed to bring the young racers to the track, and most stay to provide support and mechanical expertise in the pits.

While BMX equipment and racing expenses can be costly, the sport is no more expensive than other organized youth sports like baseball or football. Inexpensive and second-hand equipment is available, and riders can borrow helmets and other racing gear. Some tracks and parks offer low-cost racing programs, and local businesses often sponsor especially talented riders.

Regardless of who wins, BMX racing is fun. The racing scene is a social world where young riders from diverse backgrounds can compare equipment, share gear, and trade racing tips. Riders make new friends while waiting between motos and while racing on the track.

Though it is difficult to predict the sport's future, many observers believe the growth of cruiser classes and in the professional ranks throughout the world will increase spectator and rider involvement for years to come. In the pro class, they also predict new racing features that will use more difficult obstacles.

Whatever the future may bring, BMX has definitely proven itself to be more than a passing fad. It is firmly entrenched as one of today's most exciting youth sports.

Free-style jumping exhibitions are a popular activity at tracks and at skateboard parks.

Superwheels & Thrill Sports

Airplanes
  AEROBATICS
  AIRPLANE RACING
  FLYING-MODEL AIRPLANES
  HELICOPTERS
  HOME-BUILT AIRPLANES
  PERSONAL AIRPLANES
  RECORD-BREAKING AIRPLANES
  SCALE-MODEL AIRPLANES
  YESTERDAY'S AIRPLANES
  UNUSUAL AIRPLANES

Automobiles & Auto Racing
  AMERICAN RACE CAR DRIVERS
  THE DAYTONA 500
  DRAG RACING
  ICE RACING
  THE INDIANAPOLIS 500
  INTERNATIONAL RACE CAR DRIVERS
  LAND SPEED RECORD BREAKERS
  RACING YESTERDAY'S CARS
  RALLYING
  ROAD RACING
  TRACK RACING

  CLASSIC SPORTS CARS
  CUSTOM CARS
  DINOSAUR CARS: LATE GREAT CARS
    FROM 1945 TO 1966

FABULOUS CARS OF THE 1920s & 1930s
KIT CARS: CARS YOU CAN BUILD YOURSELF
MODEL CARS
RESTORING YESTERDAY'S CARS
VANS: THE PERSONALITY VEHICLES
YESTERDAY'S CARS

Bicycles
  BICYCLE MOTOCROSS RACING
  BICYCLE ROAD RACING
  BICYCLE TRACK RACING
  BICYCLES ON PARADE

Motorcycles
  GRAND NATIONAL CHAMPIONSHIP RACES
  MOPEDS: THE GO-EVERYWHERE BIKES
  MOTOCROSS MOTORCYCLE RACING
  MOTORCYCLE RACING
  MOTORCYCLES ON THE MOVE
  THE WORLD'S BIGGEST MOTORCYCLE RACE:
    THE DAYTONA 200

Other Specialties
  BALLOONING
  KARTING
  MOUNTAIN CLIMBING
  RIVER THRILL SPORTS
  SAILBOAT RACING
  SOARING
  SPORT DIVING
  SKYDIVING
  SNOWMOBILE RACING
  YESTERDAY'S FIRE ENGINES
  YESTERDAY'S TRAINS
  YESTERDAY'S TRUCKS

Lerner Publications Company
241 First Avenue North, Minneapolis, Minnesota 55401